CREMATION AND BURIAL
IN THE CONTEXT OF
CHRISTIANITY IN INDIA

CREMATION AND BURIAL IN THE CONTEXT OF CHRISTIANITY IN INDIA

Arun K Paul

ISPCK
Impacting Communities since 1710

2011

Cremation and Burial in the Context of Christianity in India –
Published by the Revd Dr Ashish Amos of the Indian Society for
Promoting Christian Knowledge (ISPCK), Post Box 1585, 1654
Madarsa Road, Kashmere Gate, Delhi-110006.

*The views expressed in the book are those of the author and the publisher
takes no responsibility for any of the statements.*

*Scriptures taken from the HOLY BIBLE, NEW INTERNATIONAL
VERSION ®. Copyright 1973, 1978, and 1984 by International Bible
Society. Used by permission of Zondervan. All rights reserved.*

ISBN : 978-81-8465-149-2

Laser typeset by
ISPCK, Post Box 1585, 1654, Madarsa Road, Kashmere Gate, Delhi-
110006.
Tel: 23866322/23
e-mail: *ashish@ispck.org.in* • *ella@ispck.org.in*
website: *www.ispck.org.in*

This work is dedicated to Rev. Dr. Chung Suk Kim for all his encouragement and support that eventually led me into the world of research and writing, and also to all those who long to see the gospel of Jesus Christ makes sense to the people of different cultures.

Contents

Acknowledgements

I am thankful to Dr. Eunice Irwin for challenging me on matters of contextual theology, and for all of her encouragement to write on this much debated but crucial issue among Christians. I am also thankful to Rev. Dr. Ashish Amos for his kindness in reading through the manuscript speedily and for expediting the process for publishing this book. Thanks to Ms. Ella Sonawane for guiding me through the publishing process. I deeply appreciate all my friends and well-wishers who read the manuscript of this book and gave me their valuable feedback. Finally, I want to thank my wife Young-Joo Shim and children, Prernna (Ria) and Prerika, for their patience as I worked on this project.

Introduction

...for dust you are and to dust you will return. — Genesis 3:19 (NIV).

Have you ever wondered what the phrase "returning to dust" means? How does a dead person "return to dust"? When the first death occurred, causing God's creation to return to dust or when He gave His commandments to the Israelites through Moses in Pentateuch, did God institute a particular mode of disposing of the dead? Does burial do any better justice to returning the dead to dust than does cremation? Can cremating the dead be considered returning the dust to dust, but with an expedited version? Are there other modes of disposing of the body in addition to burial and cremation? What makes disposing of the dead body a Christian or pagan mode? What significance does a particular practice, either cremation or burial, have? What, after all, is the meaning of this last rite in the human lifespan; does it vary from culture to culture and religion to religion? By raising these and several other related questions, the author tries to help the reader in exploring the world of tradition, history, the Scriptures and culture without losing sight of the context of this issue.

Traditionally, burial has been the norm for Christians worldwide in disposing of the body after death. Historically, Christians have considered cremation a pagan practice. However, now many Christians in countries such as the United Kingdom, the U.S.A. and South Korea opt for cremation over burial due to scarcity of land and economic and hygienic issues. In countries such as Japan and Singapore, cremation is the only available option. And for many, cremation and burial are just a matter of preference. Nevertheless, the debate continues among Christians as to whether both cremation and burial are appropriate or if burial is the only appropriate mode of disposing of the body for Christians.

In India, the burial tradition has been almost universal for Christians. It has also remained an unexamined tradition. The burial practice is considered Christian and cremation pagan. So strong are the feelings in India concerning burial versus cremation that for many what practice one has is equated with one's religious identity. Indeed, for many

Christians, cremation is tantamount to betrayal, almost an abandonment of one's Christian identity. However, the Christian burial tradition has discredited Christians from wielding an authentic Indian Christian identity. Burial stands out as an imported ritual to the Indian culture. Burying the dead is taboo for the Hindus. The practice of the burial of the dead looks foreign to Indian[1] eyes, as cremation is the widely-practiced method in funeral service. There have been instances where non-Christian Indians have avoided attending funeral services of the Christians because of the practice of burial. The increasing challenges of social pressure, scarcity of land, uncooperative neighbourhoods and biased local-government bodies have created opportunities to examine the burial custom that, in the final analysis, turns out to be more traditional than theological.

An examination of the tradition of the Christian burial reveals that the prevalent belief that burial is Christian and

---

[1] The term "non-Christian Indians" and "Indians" in this paper is used particularly to refer to Indians, regardless of various religious backgrounds, such as Sikh, Jain, Buddhist, Radha-Swami, Nirankari, etc., who practice cremation. Muslims, though they are also Indians, practice burial. This paper is strictly in the context of the majority of Indians who practice cremation as their culturally accepted mode for disposing of the dead and the term "Indians" is used in that context to refer to them.

cremation is pagan stems from a misinterpretation of the Scriptures. The study attempts to elucidate the enigma in the cremation and/or burial debate. Contextual theology of cremation will help the Christians in India to respond appropriately to the challenges posed by the burial mode. From the missiological perspective, it will also provide non-Christian Indians with an opportunity to hear the hope of resurrection for eternal life proclaimed at the Christian funeral service.

The first section of the book focuses on the need for a contextual theology of cremation. The second section discusses the Indian Christians' view on burial and cremation. This section also discusses the changes that have taken place in the attitude of some Christians towards cremation. The third section assesses the modes of the disposal of the dead. It also exposes the ignorance of the cultural context and misinterpretation of the Scriptures. The fourth section discusses how God works with cultures and customs. The fifth section describes the factors behind the spread of the burial mode. The sixth section discusses that considering one mode as superior to another is ethnocentric fallacy. The seventh section contains an analysis of the Judeo-Christian and Hindu culture perspectives on the meaning of the funeral rite and the translatability of the essence of the custom. After discussing the biblical position on resurrection in the eighth section, the author, in the ninth section, gives examples of Christians who learned the contextual theology of the modes of disposing of the body and focuses on the power of God for resurrection.

Need for a Contextual Theology of Cremation

Foreign Image of Christianity in India

While the talk of contextual theology has been gaining widespread approval in Asia, Africa and South America since the second half of the twentieth century,[1] the need for contextualisation was felt even quite earlier than that on the Indian soil in light of the increasing foreign image of

---

[1]William A. Dyrness, Veli-Matti Karkkainen, Juan Francisco Martinez and Simon Chan, eds., Global Dictionary of Theology: A Resource for the Worldwide Church (Downers Grove, Il: Inter-Varsity Press, 2008), 175-6.

Christianity. Sadhu Sunder Singh's phrase "the gospel in an Indian cup" is one of the key reflections of that spirit. Martin Alphonse is in line with H. A. Popley and V. Chakkarai in regards to the foreignness of Christianity, as he points out their views, "writing in 1920 H.A. Popley expressed his concern over the foreignness in Christianity ... and ten years later, V. Chakkarai, an outstanding Indian Christian theologian, pointed painfully to the foreignness of the Indian church...."[2] Dr. Martin Alphonse has rightly said that:

> The church in India has suffered from an image of identity crisis for long. By and large Indians consider the church to be a product and an agency of the West, imported into the nation during the colonial era. This main factor contributing to this mistaken identity of the Indian Church as a Western product has been the Western cultural flavor which has marinated many aspects of the Church's life such as its forms of worship, rituals, religious observances, administrative structure, architectural styles of buildings and so on.[3]

This foreign image has infamously vitiated the witness of the Indian Christians in their own nation. The Church in India has to make a place for itself in the hearts of Indians.

---

[2] Martin Alphonse, The Gospel for Hindus: A Study in Contextual Communication (Chennai, India: Mission Educational Books, 2003), 15.

[3] Ibid.

It must particularly emancipate Indian Christianity by identifying and discarding the foreign elements in its image. Dr. Promod Aghamkar has aptly pointed out that Jains, who are not Hindus but worshippers of Mahavira, have so well contextualised their belief system that they have established their place as Indians in contrast to Christians in India.[4]

Effects of the Theory of Functional Integration

"Functional integration is the anthropological theory in which there is interaction between every aspect of the culture. It is rare to introduce a change in one area of the culture, such as an ideology, without affecting the other areas of the culture."[5] If something new is introduced in a particular culture, it will affect the other dimensions of that culture.

An incident took place about a decade ago at the author's hometown of Manali, Himachal Pradesh. An account of this

---

[4] Promod Aghamkar, Class Lecture in "Contextual Theology". April 30, 2009.

[5] Darrell L. Whiteman, "Anthropology for Christian Mission" (Class Notes, Asbury Theological Seminary, Wilmore, KY, 1995) Quoted in Stephen Wesley Dupree, "Discovering a Contextual Model for Training Japanese for Cross-Cultural Ministry" PhD diss., Asbury Theological Seminary, Wilmore. KY, 2004. 83.

incident reflects the dynamics of the "functional integration theory." This account has also played a significant role in contemplating the contextual theology of cremation and examining the traditional Christian stand on "burial" in India.

It was a very traumatic day for Krishan Swaroop, an Indian Christian from a Brahmin family, a learned man of the Hindu scriptures. His wife suddenly died of "Bilateral Pneumonia", leaving three children behind. People from the church and his friends from the Hindu community quickly gathered in the mission hospital campus where his wife had died a short while ago. In the midst of this emotionally charged, gloomy atmosphere, one of the men from the Hindu community slowly moved towards Krishan Swaroop and leaning towards him asked, "Panditji,[6] what would you do with the body? How you are going to do the *Antim Sumskar?*"[7] Krishan Swaroop thought for a while, staring at the ground, and cast his vote in favor of burial, a mode considered Christian in India. Soon a significant number of people from the Hindu community withdrew from the scene concluding that they did not have any relationship with him.

---

[6] *Pandit Ji* is a term to address a Hindu priest.

[7] *Antim Sumskara* means the last rite, it is a term used for funeral ceremony.

There is a famous saying in India that "if you don't go to a person's wedding that is fine, but you must attend a funeral service or go to console the family in bereavement."

Dr. Subhash C. Sharma says:

Traditionally, whenever there was a death in the community, a male person belonging to each household—irrespective of the caste—would attend the funeral to pay respects to the dead. Moreover, everyone going to the crematorium on such an occasion would carry some wood with him to add to the pyre. This was to assist in gathering the necessary fuel for cremation.[8]

Now, cremation in the Indian context, where the pyre is a large pile of wood that is mostly brought or carried by the people, shows a sense of respect to the deceased and his or her family, as Dr. Subhash Sharma described above.

In this social context, Krishan Swaroop had, sadly, lost all the comfort and relationship he had with those people from the Hindu community who once must have been his friends. And the ones who left had lost the privilege to hear the message of the hope of resurrection and eternal life preached at the Christian funeral service.

---

[8] Subhash C. Sharma, "Cremation and Its Origin in Hinduism." 2008. *http://seva.sulekha.com/blog/post/2008/03/cremation-and-its-origin-in-hinduism.htm* (accessed December 30, 2009).

Scarcity of Space: Uncooperative Society and Biased Government

There are two other reasons for the need of contextual theology: (1) the scarcity of space and (2) the current religio-political situation in India. Pro-Hindu state governments, in some states, come under the pressure of religious fanatics who impede the process for acquiring land for the cemeteries. In 2003, the author's local church was in the process of getting a piece of land, since the little Anglican Church cemetery at Manali had been filled long before. At times, believers had even dug some of the old graves, those without any epithets, and reburied the remains using a little space so that the new dead body could be buried. Finally, though the government officials showed the church leaders a piece of land by the river side for burial, the process was halted as the nearby village claimed the land for village affairs. The author's church still does not have a piece of land that could be used for burial.

The metropolitan cities in India are facing a crisis related to the scarcity of space for burial. In the case of Chennai, Tamil Nadu, "the Madras Cemeteries Board (MCB), which is managing the operations of three old cemeteries in the city, has proposed the cremation of Christians in view of space crunch in the cemeteries."[9] An incident in Manipur, a North-eastern State in India, sheds light on the situation that Christians face in their social relationship with others due to the burial issue:

> Imphal, Manipur: Christian minorities of Huikap village have been ordered by the village authorities not to bury their dead in the village nor carry the dead bodies through it. Violation of the order would result in dire consequences, they have been warned. According to sources reaching the All India Christian Council, Manipur branch, the trouble started when a two-year-old Christian boy drowned in a village pond and died. The body was buried July 19 in a plot donated by a family from a neighboring Christian village. The ground was to serve as a cemetery for the Christians. However, soon after the boy's burial, the child's father and the pastor of the local church were summoned by the Huikap villagers and were forced to sign a document promising they would remove the boy's body by 10 a.m. July 20, the AICC sources said. After persistent requests, the villager authorities though relented, but issued a stern warning that no Christian dead body would be allowed to be buried nor carried through the village. Christians allege that since the incident took place,

---

[9] "Chennai Christians Consider Cremation" [2004]; *http://www.indiamike.com/india/india-travel-news-and-commentary-f80/chennai-christians-consider-cremation-t7813/#post58849* (Accessed September 4, 2009)

they were being harassed by the village authorities who called them every night over the issue.[10]

The pro-burial approach has failed to address this issue of concern to Christians in India. Bouillard's comments are aptly fitting here, "a theology that is not somehow reflective of our times, our culture, and our current concerns—and so contextual—is also a false theology."[11] This leads us to the realisation that Indian Christians need a contextual theology of cremation to cope with the growing challenges against the practicality of burial in various contexts discussed here.

---

[10] Sar News, "Don't bury your dead here, Manipuri village heads warn Christians," *http://www.indiancatholic.in/news/storydetails.php/12811-1—Don%E2%80%99t-bury-your-dead-here,-Manipuri-village-heads-warn-Christians.* (accessed September 4, 2009)

[11] Stephen B. Bevans, Models of Contextual Theology (Maryknoll, New York: Orbis Books, 2005), 5.

2

Christian Identity in the Indian Context: Cremation or Burial

A majority of Indian Christians do not feel free to choose between cremation and burial as a mode of disposing of the body. Burial is observed as the normal and traditional Christian practice for Indian Christians and to cremate the dead is to deny one's Christian identity. A little research into the matter reveals that Indian Christians do not have clarity on this subject.

The author interviewed a new believer coming from a Sikh family and asked him, "What should be done with your body at your death, in terms of cremation and burial?" He confidently answered, "Now I am a Christian, so I would be buried...the Bible talks about burial and Jesus was also buried and resurrected."[1] In conversation with Indian Christians, both layman and clergy, the author heard a majority of them denouncing cremation as pagan and elevating burial as a mark of Christian identity. James W. Frazer, a Baptist pastor and a pro-burial advocate, records a similar answer in his query. He writes,

> I asked a missionary from India if the Christians of that land cremated their dead. With a look of surprise he said, "Positively not! Cremation is heathen. The Christians of India bury their dead because burial is Christian." There is absolutely nothing Christian about cremation; it is as pagan as idol worship.[2]

An almost identical response was received by Rev. Mark Creech from an Indian pastor who said that cremation was but "an ancient practice of heathen origins."[3]

---

[1] Tejpal Bajwa, Interview by Author, phone call, March 7, 2009.

[2] James W. Fraser, Cremation: Is it Christian? (Neptune, New Jersey: Loizeaux Brothers, 1965), 15.

[3] Mark Creech, "Is Cremation Christian?," in The Raleigh Herald, 2002, http://www.worldnewspaperpublishing.com/News/FullStory.asp?loc=TRW&ID=367 (accessed May 1, 2009).

Interestingly, when the author questioned some individuals in regards to their theological basis for ascribing a mode as either "pagan" or "Christian", and what will happen to those Christians who have been cremated out of necessity, i.e., hygienic burning to control contagious diseases, those martyred by being burned alive or those who accidentally succumbed to death by fire, the pro-burial individuals appeared to have no idea of any theologically appropriate answer. They hold their argument basically on the traditional view of Christianity:

- The Bible records the burial mode as the normal way of disposing of the dead body with the hope of resurrection; Jesus was also buried in a tomb and was resurrected.

- The thought of cremating the body has the Hindu, pagan connotation with all its meanings contrary to Christian faith.

There are still others who have been so accustomed to the traditions that they can not think otherwise. Rev. Zhabu Teruja, General Secretary, Nagaland Baptist Church Council, said, "I cannot imagine going to a crematorium though I think of late some protestant churches are showing leniency on this matter, honoring the wishes of the individual. A person may opt for cremation due to some genuine reasons but it is not acceptable to tradition."[4]

There also have been glimpses of those who think there is no difference between cremation and burial for a Christian. But they probably do not have the sources to present their view in a way that would convince others about their position. For example, a pastor who wishes to remain unnamed said, "The matter of resurrection is really unimportant...for cremation hastens the same process that takes place with a body over a long period of time."[5] But it is important to note here, that the pastor wanted to remain unnamed while making this comment. This clearly demonstrates that the clergy themselves are not sure how to examine this tradition in order to grasp the truth and present it to the laity. Gautam Siddharth, writer of the article "Christians taking to cremation in a big way," is quite right in saying that "there has been considerable debate among Christians on cremation, but it has been in hushed tones for fear of breaking age-old conventions."[6]

---

[4] Gautam Siddharth, "Christians taking to cremation in a big way." *http://timesofindia.indiatimes.com/articleshow/msid-2374986,prtpage-1.cms* (accessed September 4, 2009).

[5] Siddharth.

[6] *Ibid.*

While there has been a great deal of reluctance among the Protestant Christians in regards to cremation, the Catholics there have begun to talk in favor of cremation. Father Dominic Emmanuel, Delhi Archdiocese, said, "I wouldn't say we are actively pursuing cremation of bodies, but, yes, we are suggesting that the Church has absolutely no objection to cremation."[7] A thorough investigation of this issue is needed to inform Indian Christians of the Bible-based Christian position. The next section deals with this investigation.

---

[7] *Ibid.*

3

Modes of Disposing of the Dead

In the investigation, the first step is to briefly explore the history of disposing of a corpse. While there are various modes of disposing of the dead, there are different factors, such as social, cultural and circumstantial, that influence the changes in these modes. Various cultures have practiced various modes of disposing of the dead, most with a variety of attached meanings. "Burial in the earth in a man made grave, barrow or cairn is another ancient form…burning of the body…less common or less well-known modes of disposition are water burial, simple exposure to the elements, preservation of the body in a quasi-dwelling and cannibalism."[1]

Archeologists believe that the burial mode is most likely the oldest mode of disposing of the dead, as Dr. E. O. James, professor of history of religion, based on the research in archeological field, places the burial ritual as the intentional mode of disposing of a body, in the Paleolithic age (i.e., the earliest period of the Stone Age). His idea is that cremation was rather unintentional: "In many cases it would seem that bodies were burnt accidentally as a result of purificatory fires having been lighted in graves, or for the purpose of desiccating the corpse."[2]

Archeological research in the villages bordering the Indus civilisation points out that, among various methods of interment, "fractional" burial was popular in the third millennium B.C.[3] In the second millennium B.C., both cremation and inhumation were in practice by the Indo-European invaders. A funeral hymn in *Rig-Veda*, which has an appeal to the fire god, Agni, not to consume the deceased

---

[1] Paul Irion, Cremation (Philadelphia: Fortress Press, 1968), 2.

[2] E.O. James, Prehistoric Religion (New York: Barnes and Noble, 1963), 98.

[3] James, 247.

but to bring the dead to maturity, and an appeal to send the deceased "on his way to the Fathers."[4] Suggestively, due to this funeral hymn cremation would have played its role[5] in disposing of the body.

Beginning in the Stone Age, this practice eventually spread throughout the ancient world and was not resisted, except by a few cultures.[6] The Egyptians, of course, developed various processes for preserving the body by embalming it. The Chinese constantly buried their dead, and the Jews gradually changed from cave sepulchre to earth burial. The Babylonians practiced both cremation and burial in a process where they collected ashes in clay jars pointing to the belief that there was the continuing presence of the spirit of the dead. It is believed that the practice of cremation came to ancient Greece from the North around 1000 B.C. Though it did not fully replace the burial custom of Mycenaean culture, it did make its place in the culture among the Greeks.[7] A likely reason for this particular practice is believed to be the issue of health, "Plato urged

---

[4] James, 248.

[5] *Ibid.*

[6] Irion, 5.

[7] *Ibid.*

that burials not be made at fields under cultivation...at the time of Pericles a plague resulted in many deaths, and the use of cremation as a sanitary means was encouraged."[8]

This brief account reveals that there were various modes of disposing of the dead and burial and cremation both were practiced widely. Interestingly, pagans were also practicing burial. Hittite, the so-called pagan, from whom Abraham bought a piece of land and the cave in it to bury Sarah, also shared the same custom of burying the dead (Gen. 23:6-11). If we use the mode of burial to determine what is and what is not pagan, we would inacurately conclude that the Chinese and the Hittites were not pagan. It is not simply the mode of burial but the meaning attached to the mode that makes the ritual pagan. Despite both cultures maintaining the mode of burial, the Chinese are recognised as "pagan" due to ancestral worship and the Hittites for not worshipping YHWH. Alfred C. Rush, in the context of burial, says that the distinction between pagan and Christian concepts was due to the underlying belief expressed at death rituals: "However, where the cult of the dead in ancient times was linked with the pagan concept of death, or where it bordered on idolatry, there the separation of Christianity

---

[8] *Ibid.*, 5-6.

from ancient culture began. The pagan mourning practices were supplanted by the singing of psalms. Crowning the dead after the manner of gods and idols was rejected."[9]

Burial Is More Cultural Than Theological

There are precisely two main arguments against cremation from the pro-burial point of view. The first is the biblical account of burial and cremation, and the second, God's anger against the practice of cremation as noted in certain scriptures. But both of these arguments reflect that the Christian interpretation has completely missed the point on two grounds: (1) ignorance of the "cultural context" and (2) inability to fully understand the "Scriptural context." The result of all this is false theology.

Ignorance of the Cultural Context

The biblical account of burial and cremation falls into the following categories:

- Traditionally-approved examples of burial in the Bible,

- Traditionally-negative examples of cremation in the Bible

---

[9]Alfred C. Rush, "Death and Burial in Christian Antiquity" (Ph.D. Diss., The Catholic University of America Press, Washington, D.C., 1941), viii.

Traditionally-Approved Examples of Burial in the Bible

Rev. James Frazer, a leading figure for the pro-burial view, points out that there are biblical examples of funeral that record that the Hebrews normally practiced burial by interment or inhumation and that Jesus himself was buried.[10] Rev. James Frazer speaks of all the positive examples in the Bible in relation to burial; his special emphasis is on "Joseph's bones" (Exod. 13:19) for which Moses takes the trouble to bring them to the promised land in order to bury forty years later (Josh. 24:32). In addition, based on the event of God burying Moses (Deut. 34:5-8), Frazer strongly argues, "Why did God bury Moses? He could have disposed of his body in many other ways. Burial is the only God-given way of honorably disposing of the body."[11]

Traditionally-Negative Examples of Cremation in the Bible

In the Bible, cremation is shown as something negative, as it was used to demonstrate punishment. Examples of this

---

[10] John J. Davis, What About Cremation: A Christian Perspective (Winona Lake, Indiana: BMH Books, 1989), 12.

[11] Fraser, 13.

negative point of view are Achan's sin (Joshua 7:15, 25) and penalties related to sexual promiscuity (Lev. 20:14; 21:9).[12] In the context of Hebrew culture, cremation had a negative connotation. Thus, these records point to the validity of "burial" as the traditionally-accepted mode by God's people.

Both of these aforementioned points against the mode of cremation fall short before the counter examination in the context of cultural influence. Biblical accounts in support of the mode of burial as the Christian mode are in the context of Hebrew culture. Christianity was born in the lap of the Hebrew cultural context, and this is the fact that cannot be ignored. The first followers of Jesus were culturally Jewish.[13] Definitely, the Hebrew culture had a significant effect on the first Christians. "Christians in Jewish communities continued with the custom of sepulcher or burial"[14] Even Hebrews themselves were influenced by the Egyptians in the method of embalming. This was never practiced in Israel but "the two examples known, those of Jacob and Joseph, are explicitly ascribed to Egyptian custom (Gen. 50:2-3)."[15]

---

[12] Davis, 64.

[13] *Ibid.*, 12.

[14] Irion, 9.

[15] Roland de Vaux, Ancient Israel: Social Institutions Vol.1 (New York: McGraw-Hill Book Company, 1965), 56.

The Egyptian culture even had this influence on Christians since "Coptic Christians in Egypt retained the practice of mummification"[16]

Similarly, the question put up by Rev. James Frazer, "Why God buried Moses?" must be understood in the context of immediate Hebrew culture and custom. It is quite probable that God used the culture of the Hebrews, as it was natural to them: burial was the honorable mode and cremation had negative connotations.

Misinterpretation of the Scriptural Context

Another argument against cremation is the text in the Book of Amos. Pro-burial advocates take it to be an example of God's anger against the practice of cremation in the Scriptures. Frazer thinks that God punished Moab for this grave sin and he even uses the phrase "unpardoned sin."[17] Frazer quoted Amos chapter 2 verse 1: "Thus saith the Lord: for three transgressions of Moab…will not turn away punishment…because he burned the bones of the king of Edom into lime."[18] And, he interpreted this scripture as God's direct disapproval of the practice of cremation.[19]

---

[16] Irion, 9.
[17] Fraser, 14.
[18] *Ibid.*
[19] *Ibid.*

But a close examination of the context tells a different story. Frazer's interpretation of chapter 2 verse 1 that it was "God's direct command against cremation" is misinterpretation of the Scripture. Though the main examples of cremation in the Old Testament are used in the context of punishment, the overall context of the aforementioned text of Amos has nothing to do with identifying the doctrine of cremation as pagan. The dominant theme, in the context of the Scripture here is "social injustice and idolatry" that leads to God's judgment. The immediate context of the Amos Scripture is actually in a series of judgments: God is speaking against various nations, including Judah and Israel, due to their social injustice and cruelty done to others in the first two chapters. God's punishment comes on Moab not because of their cremating the king of Edom but in the context of the demonstration of extreme cruelty on the former's part.

Culture, Customs and God

Biblical records, as we have seen in the last section, do not explicitly talk about whether God endorsed certain customs or rituals. However, there is also scriptural evidence to show that God works with people in the cultural worldview they know and understand. Books like Exodus, Leviticus and Deuteronomy are teeming with God's commandments on a variety of issues about his people in terms of their relationship with God and with each other. But God did not give explicit commandments to His people in regards to each and everything they were supposed to do. In addition, God did not remake all the customs for them to live by, and He did not communicate certain aspects of these customs to them.

According to the Biblical records, God seemed to be working with people right in their cultural context and the customs they were already familiar with, as in the case with the covenants. Passages in Genesis and Jeremiah (Gen. 15:7-21; Jer. 34:18)[1] point towards the clarification that passing through the halves of slaughtered animals must have been the common practice to enact a covenant between the two parties. God employed the use of this practice to make and state his covenant with His people. In many cases, "the covenants of the Bible resemble other legal documents of the Ancient Near East."[2]

During the days of the Judges (Ruth 4:7), removing the sandal and giving it to the other person was the custom to confirm the deal in Israel. However, this practice was never mentioned as being part of God's law to the Hebrews to confirm the deal; though there is a reference in Deut. 25:8-10 that pretty much sounds similar. However, that is in the context of failing to perform the marriage duty by the brother of the deceased man. In Deuteronomy, it is to

---

[1] New International Version

[2] Geoffery Wigoder, *The New Encyclopedia of Judaism*, (New York: New York University Press, 2002), 187.

embarrass the one who refuses to marry his dead brother's wife in order to continue his brother's name in Israel (See detail in context, Deut. 25: 5-10). The widow would remove his sandal and spit in his face.

In another instance, it must have been the custom of the people that the married women would give their maidservants to their husbands to procreate, while they were unable to conceive. Sarah gave Hagar to Abraham (Gen. 16:1-4) and Leah and Rachel gave their maidservants to Jacob for procreation (Gen. 30). Interestingly, God did not reject those ideas either directly or indirectly but worked through them. This is even expressed in the example of buying slaves. From the Scripture it is clear that God is not initiating the custom or culture of buying slaves nor is He the originator of slavery. Even so, God does not denounce the practice, but simply instructs His people in terms of how they should treat a slave when they buy him (Exod. 21:1-11). However, God is not silent when there is need to comment.

It is important to note that God is not so passive about cultures and customs that He does not bother to comment. Though God seemed to be working with people in their own context with the method people understood, He is particular in pointing out when certain customs are evil.

There are cases where God says that He abhors things and commands his people to reject them. For instance, God abhors offering children to Molech in sacrifice (Lev. 20:1-5). Other situations include the customs and practices of other nations, particularly the Canaanites (20:22-23).

It is important to note that there is no direct or indirect comment against cremation and funeral customs in general in the Bible. Assuming that burial is on the same level as other decrees that God makes is nothing short of a huge error of adding to the Bible. As Stephen Prothero also comments that there is no definitive "Thus saith the Lord" as far as the question of burial versus cremation is concerned.[3]

---

[3] Stephen Prothero, Purified by Fire: A History of Cremation in America (Los Angeles: University of California Press, 2001), 78.

Factors behind the Spread of the Burial Mode

Influence of the First Hebrew Christians

As noted earlier, the first Christians were Hebrew and culturally burial was the appropriate mode of disposing of the body while burning was associated with punishment. It is possible that they may have even influenced the gentile Christians against cremation.

Burial of Jesus and Hope of Resurrection

Jesus' burial and resurrection might have been a strong stimulation for early Christians to imitate burial in the hope for resurrection; since "the symbolism of the body at rest in the grave may have been a significant context for belief in the resurrection."[1]

Burial Distinguished Christians from Pagans

Early Christians were persecuted and their bodies were guarded so that they would not be buried. This was because burial was associated with the Christian faith of resurrection. In those situations, after some days, the bodies were burned.[2] In this context, when the bodies of the early Christians were thus disrespected it was Tertullian, a Christian apologist and church father, who spoke in regards to this treatment as cruelty and punishment and favored burial[3] as the distinguished mode. The Christians resisted cremation as it also had its pagan association in form and implications in the pagan cultures.[4] Speaking about the first few centuries before the legalisation of Christianity under Constantine, Paul Irion says, "The mode of burial became

---

[1] *Ibid.*, 10.

[2] The Church History of Eusibius, Bk. V, chap. 1. Quoted in Paul Irion, Cremation (Philadelphia: Fortress Press, 1968), 10.

[3] Tertullian, De Anima, 51. Quoted in Paul Irion, Cremation (Philadelphia: Fortress Press, 1968), 11.

[4] Irion, 15.

one of the significant marks that distinguished the Christians from the pagans in these centuries."[5]

Legalisation of Christianity under Christian Rulers

Under Constantinople, Christianity was legalised. The influence of the Church was so strong that the practice of burial became more prevalent; and "by the end of the fifth century burial superseded cremation in the Christian world."[6] Towards the end of the eighth century another solid step was taken against the practice of cremation: "The emperor Charlemagne criminalized cremation in the Christian west in 789 AD."[7]

Influence of Missionaries in the Colonial Era

The diffusion of Christianity during the colonial era by Euro-Western missionaries, along with their cultural baggage, has greatly influenced Indians' cultural life. Under the cultural influence of the Euro-Western missionaries, the Indian Christians began to bury their dead. While burial became the accepted Christian funeral practice, cremation

---

[5] *Ibid.*, 11.

[6] *Ibid.*, 12.

[7] Douglas J. Davies and Lewis H. Mate Eds, Encyclopedia of Cremation. (Burlington: Ashgate Publishing Company, 2005), xviii.

was denounced as pagan and thus un-Christian among the Indian Christians. In 1884, when two newly-baptised Indian Christians were cremated the vicar apostolic of Vizagapatam (sic) raised the issue as to what should be the Church's response in the situation when the pagan seek baptism at the deathbed. His conclusion was "do not approve of cremation, but be passive in the matter and always confer baptism."[8]

Nepal, a nation dominated by the Hindus, has been a hard place to live for Christians. They have tried to maintain their Christian identity by defending the burial mode as the Christian mode. Dr. Bal Krishna Sharma's comments reflect the picture Christianity has in Nepal, as he says that "exactly why Nepalese Christians insist on burying is an open issue that raises questions over the potential influence of missionaries and their own traditional burial practices as well as the need to assert a Christian identity over and against the Hindu-Buddhist approach to religion, life and death."[9]

---

[8] *Ibid.*, 108.

[9] *Ibid.*, 326.

One Mode as Superior to the Other: An Ethnocentric Fallacy

The issue of cremation and burial is so culturally conditioned that to hold on to one view over the other is an obvious ethnocentric perspective. Two contrasting views on the barbarousness of burial and cremation are evidence to this thesis. James Frazer says, "A great many refined people shrink from consigning the bodies of loved ones to destruction by the process of cremation, because of its apparent inhuman and pagan aspect. After all, the custom was handed down from the barbarous people of the dark ages. Most certainly it is inhuman and godless, to say at least."[1] On the contrary, for a Hindu burial is barbarous. A Hindu scholar objects to burial saying:

> Cremation or burning of the dead body is the most recognized mode of the disposal of corpse among the Hindus from the time of the Vedas up to the present day. This mode evolved at a high stage of the human civilization, as it is the most scientific and refined.[2]

What people accept as normal and good is largely the result of peoples' views that are conditioned by their culture and religion. A great example is in the case of disposing the dead in Zoroastrianism. "The prescribed method of disposal of the dead in Zoroastrianism is by exposure to wild birds and animals and the 'purifying rays of the sun' initially on rock in uninhabited places and later in special stone buildings called 'towers of silence' (dakhmas)."[3] Though the meaning of the death rite in Zoroastrianism has its own context, the cultural conditioning of this religion has made the followers recognise this mode as the only normal way of disposing of

---

[1] Fraser, 16.

[2] Pandey, Hindu Samskaras: Socio Religious Study of the Hindu Sacraments (Delhi: Motilal Banarsidass, 1969) 241.

[3] Davies, Douglas J., with Mates, Lewis H. Encyclopedia of Cremation. (Aldershot: Ashgate Publishing Ltd., 2006), 429.

the dead. Charles Kraft has aptly made the point that it is cultural conditioning that has a great influence on man's perception of reality:

> There is always a difference between reality and human culturally conditioned understandings (models) of the reality. We assume that there is a reality "out there" but it is the mental constructs (models) of that reality inside our heads that are the most real to us. God, the author of reality, exists outside any culture. Human beings, on the other hand, are always bound by culture, subculture (including disciplinary), and psychological conditioning to perceive and interpret what they see of reality in ways appropriate to these conditionings. Neither the absolute God nor the reality [God] created is perceived absolutely by culture-bound human beings.[4]

A discussion on the religio-cultural meaning or the principle of the death rite, along with its mode of disposing of the dead is necessary in order to discover the elements that make the whole death ritual so significant for those inside the culture.

---

[4] Charles H. Kraft. Christianity in Culture. (Maryknoll, NY: Orbis Books, 1979), 300. Quoted in Stephen Bevans, Models of Contextual Theology (Maryknoll, NY: Orbis Books, 2005) 4.

Translatability of the Essence of the Custom: An Analysis

Culture Matters

Today many of the customs of one culture are not appropriate for other culture(s). For example if the Apostle Paul's exhortation in the context of Greek culture (1 Corinthians 16:20) is taken directly into the context of the Indian Church, "Greet one another with a holy kiss," it would have a disastrous affect on the image of Christianity in India as an immoral religion, and, eventually, rejection by the masses. Though we are sure that it is God's Word for all cultures we do not take this exhortation literally, but look for the principles behind the culturally conditioned practice.

Even in the case of the "holy kiss", in the Greek culture, there are instances where a warm greeting, not the kiss, is expressed to acquaintances, and not to strangers.[1] Christians in India would have to come up with a culturally appropriate expression of "warm Christian love" towards each other, which might be simply joining hands with a little bow in the gesture or shaking hands, or even by hugging each other, but only with the person of the same gender. Thus, the essence will remain and the Word of God will have its meaning for the people in their own cultural context.

Judeo-Christian Perspective on the Meaning of Funeral Rite

Since the early Christians were Jews, they were influenced by Hebrew culture. It is important to see the meaning of the funeral rite in Hebrew culture. This rite focuses on two fundamental aspects, namely 'respect for the body of the deceased' and the 'spiritual meaning of the mode.' Roland de Vaux's study of the death and funeral rites of ancient Hebrews shows that a special honor and a spiritual value was attached to the burial custom:

---

[1] N.d. "How Do People Greet Each Other in Greek?" *http://wiki.answers.com/Q/How_do_people_greet_each_other_in_Greek,* (accessed September 2, 2009).

The distinction between soul and body is something foreign to the Hebrew mentality, and death, therefore, is regarded as the separation of these two elements. A live man is a living 'soul' (nephesh), and a dead man is a dead 'nephesh' (Nb 6:6; Lv 21:11; cf. Nb 19:13). Death is not annihilation. So long as the body exists and the bones at least remain, the soul exists, like a shade, in a condition of extreme weakness, in the subterranean abode of sheol (Jb26:5-6; Is14:9-10; Ez 32:17-32). The ideas account for the care bestowed on the corpse and the importance of honorable burial, for the soul continued to feel what was done to the body. Hence to be left unburied, a prey to the birds and the wild beasts, was the worst of all curses (1 Kings 14:11; Jr 16:4; 22:19; Ez 29:5).[2]

Since early Christians had embraced Hebrew culture they continued following the burial custom but with the profound addition of resurrection hope.

Hindu Culture Perspective on Meaning of Funeral Rite

All the rites and ceremonies related to death imply the two main beliefs held by the Hindus regarding the proper disposal of the dead—the dignity of the human body and liberation of the soul from the attachment to the body for reincarnation. "Until these rites and ceremonies are duly

---

[2] de Vaux, 56.

performed, the soul of man is not finally dismissed to its place in the next world... The Hindus even now regard cremation as absolutely necessary for the welfare of the souls of the dead...Unless the ceremony is performed, the departed soul is believed to linger about its late habitation and hover without consolation, and in great distress as a Preta [a ghost]."[3] A fresh example of this twofold belief is in the protest by Davender Ghai, an Indian living in Britain, who demanded the High Court allow him to have an open-air cremation. The title of the news story was "A Hindu man has told the High Court he wants to die 'with dignity' and not to be 'bundled into a box' in a case to retain open-air cremations."[4] He says, "Being bundled into a box and incinerated in a furnace is not my idea of dignity, much less the performance of an ancient sacrament."[5] According to a British Broadcasting Corporation report:

> Davender Ghai, 70, a devout Hindu, wants to overturn a Newcastle Council decision preventing funeral pyres being

---

[3] Pandey, 243.

[4] BBC News "Hindu fights for pyre 'dignity'" *http://news.bbc.co.uk/go/pr/fr/-/2/hi/uk_news/england/7960489.stmPublished: 2009/03/24* 13:54:13 GMT (accessed March 26, 2009).

[5] *Ibid.*

held in line with religious practice. Mr Ghai insists that the process is essential to free the soul after death... "As a Hindu, I believe my soul should be liberated in consecrated fire, 'Agni', after death—a sacramental rebirth, like the mythical phoenix arising from the flames anew," he said.[6]

From the analysis of these two cultural modes, Hebrew burial and Hindu cremation, along with the meaning attached to the death rite, there emerge two main points concerning the disposal of the dead: (1) honoring the body and (2) the spiritual meaning attached to the body. Coleman has rightly said that "Whatever we say about funerals really pivots on our view of the importance of the body."[7]

---

[6] *Ibid.*

[7] William L. Coleman, It's Your Funeral (Wheaton, Illinois: Tyndale House Publishers, 1979) 19.

Resurrection and Biblical Position

Burial Is Not a Criterion for Resurrection

The view that burial is related to resurrection is popularly held by the Christians in general. It is more plausible to relate resurrection to burial than to cremation. Apostle Paul's references to the laying of the body in the earth, (1Cor.15:42-44; cf. v. 37) as sowing seed that will ultimately be raised makes sense considering inhumation.[1] Similarly, the image used in the first epistle to Thessalonians, where the dead are referred to as people who are sleeping, makes

---

[1] Davis, 85-6.

more sense in relation to resurrection (1 Cor. 15:51 cf. 1 Thess. 4:13-18).[2]

However, it would be quite illogical and biased to make a doctrine of resurrection based on the idea of burial. There have been countless cases in human history where Christians—laymen, clergymen, Bible teachers, missionaries and theologians—were either burned alive due to persecution, cremated at death, favoured cremation, or voluntarily chose cremation for practical reasons yet with the hope of resurrection.

Indian Christians are not unaware of the tragic incident that took place in the state of Orissa in 1999, when an Australian missionary named Graham Staines and his two sons were burned alive by Hindu extremists, while sleeping in their vehicle.[3] Sadly, there recently have been additional attacks on Christians in the state of Orissa.[4] Several years

---

[2] *Ibid.*

[3] BBC News "South Asia Thousands mourn missionary's death." *http://news.bbc.co.uk/2/hi/south_asia/261391.stm*. Accessed on September 2, 2009.

[4] IBN Live "Paralytic burnt alive in Kandhamal Violence." *http://ibnlive.in.com/news/paralytic-burnt-alive-in-kandhamal-voilence/75439-3.html*. Accessed on September 2, 2009.

ago, a Nepali Christian in Manali, a town in Northern India, was cremated following a lack of land in the old Anglican cemetery in the area.[5] A noted Bible teacher G. Campbell Morgan spoke in favor of cremation: "As to cremation there is certainly nothing in scripture to forbid it. We need to remember that cremation is the hastening of the process that would take time through burial. Personally, I am in favor of cremation, and it does not invalidate any biblical view of personality."[6]

Twentieth-century Methodist Christian missionary and theologian E. Stanley Jones had a hope of resurrection in the power of God more than in the mode of disposing of the dead body when he instructed his daughter, Eunice Matthews, to choose between either modes in the context of practicality in relation to his death. He did not have to accept burial as Christian and reject cremation as pagan. His conversations with his daughter speak to that hope. He

---

[5]Author's Personal Witness

[6]Jil Morgan, ed. This Was His Faith (New York: Revell, 1952): pp.243-54, quoted in John J. Davis, What About Cremation: A Christian Perspective (Winona Lake, Indiana: BMH Books, 1989), 84.

was cremated so that it could be easier to bring him (i.e., his ashes) to Baltimore for burial.[7]

> After his [E. Stanley Jones] paralytic stroke I [Eunice Matthew] asked him 'If you should die what do you want us to do with your body?' He said, 'If I die in the country [USA] I want to be buried in Baltimore cemetery and if I die in India I want to be cremated and want half of my ashes kept in Sut-taal ashram and half to be put in Baltimore cemetery'; close to the church, then called 'memorial church,' that is where he was converted.[8]

Hope of Resurrection Not Resuscitation

Christians need to understand that the concept of resurrection is absolutely different from the idea of resuscitation. In resuscitation, the old physical body is required to bring the life back into it in order to live again, but ultimately to die, sooner or later. The Bible records several examples where the people were brought to life in the same body but not for eternity. Elisha raised the son of a widow (2 Kings 4:18-38); Jesus raised the son of a widow (Luke 7:11-15); and Jesus raised Lazarus four days after his

---

[7] Eunice Matthews. *Phone* Interview by Author, May 14, 2009.
[8] *Ibid.*

death (John 11:38-44). "Life was prolonged but not indefinitely. Death was postponed but not cancelled."[9]

However, the resurrection of Jesus Christ inaugurated the concept of the "glorious body" (Phil. 3:21). The body that Jesus had after his resurrection had no place for aging, dying and putrefying.[10] In talking about the order of events at the second coming of the Lord, Paul says that those who are alive would not precede the dead.

> For the Lord himself will come down from heaven, with a loud command, with the voice of the archangel and with the trumpet call of God, and the dead in Christ will rise first. After that, we who are still alive. and are left will be caught up together with them in the clouds to meet the Lord in the air. And so we will be with the Lord forever (1 Thess. 4:16-17 [NIV]).

While the epistle to the Thessalonians describes the order well, the epistle to the Corinthians describes the change that is going to take place at resurrection.

> Listen, I tell you a mystery: We will not all sleep, but we will all be changed—in a flash, in the twinkling of an eye, at the last trumpet. For the trumpet will sound, the dead will be raised imperishable, and we will be changed (1 Cor. 15:51-52 [NIV]).

---

[9] J. David Pawson, Explaining The Resurrection (Kent, England: Sovereign World, 1993), 8.

[10] *Ibid.*, 9, 54.

And the change is into the "glorious body" as the Lord Jesus Himself has (Phil. 3:21). The important point is that this hope of resurrection with the new, spiritual, glorious, imperishable and immortal body (1 Cor. 15:44-54) is for all "the dead in Christ." What David Pawson says about resurrection is the summary of this discussion:

> One thing is clear—resurrection is about bodies. It is to be re-embodied. Other resuscitations bring people back to life in their old bodies, only to die again. However, for Jesus, resurrection meant going on life, in a new body, never to die again.[11]

In conclusion, Christians can employ the mode of cremation to dispose of the dead body, with the manner of respect and assured hope for resurrection in accordance with the Word of God. Resurrection is the hope that supersedes all modes of disposing of the dead body. This hope has its roots in the resurrection power of God and is not limited to a particular mode, as in the most popular assumption of burial.

---

[11] Pawson, 9.

9

Lessons to Be Learned: Freedom of Choice

Examples Drawn from the Early Church

Examples drawn from the early Church shed light on the fact that the believers did not seem to concern themselves as to how their bodies should be disposed of after their death. The early Church's hope of resurrection was simply in trusting God for His resurrection power, regardless of the mode of disposing of the dead body. St. Ignatius the Martyr, writing to the Romans, showed his faith in God for resurrection.

Suffer me to be eaten by the beasts, through whom I may attain to God. I am God's wheat, and I am ground by the teeth of wild beasts that I may be found pure bread of Christ. Rather entice the wild beasts that they may become my tomb and leave no trace of my body that when I fall asleep I be not burdensome to any. Then I truly be a disciple of Jesus Christ when the world shall not even see my body.[1]

Titian expressed his faith when he said, "And though dispersed through rivers and seas or torn in pieces by wild beasts, I am laid up in the storehouse of a wealthy Lord...yet God the sovereign when He so wishes will restore the substance that is visible to Him alone to its former state."[2] Thus, in the face of such examples, Stephen Prothero appropriately states that putting cremation as a stumbling block to resurrection is challenging the omnipotence of God.[3] The power of God can resurrect both a body decayed by burial and a body burned to ashes, scattered and dissolved in the atmosphere.

Lesson from Euro-Western and South-East-Asian Christians

Christians in Euro-Western and in some South-East-Asian countries have learnt to do theology in the context of the

---

[1] Rush, 84.

[2] *Ibid.*

[3] Prothero, 84.

challenges posed by war, space, hygiene and economic issues. World War II brought the greatest change in England's attitudes to cremation "because the government then recognized its critical space problem and began to promote cremation."[4] The Journal of the Cremation Society of Great Britain and the International Cremation Federation show that in 1988, "approximately 70% of British cremations compared with 15% in the U.S.A., 31% in Canada, 43% in Holland and 57% in Switzerland."[5] After eight years, in 1996, according to other statistics recorded by Stephen Prothero, Professor of Religion, Boston University,[6] the U.S. cremation rate reached just about 22% and by 1999 it reached 25%.[7]

According to researchers, there are at least six trends that are affecting the growth of cremation in the United States:[8] Society is becoming middle aged, the education

---

[4] Coleman, 58.

[5] "The Journal of the Cremation Society of Great Britain and the International Cremation Federation," Pharos International [1989] Vol. 5. No. 4. Quoted in J. Douglas Davies, Cremation Today and Tomorrow (Bramcote, Nottingham: Grove Books Limited, 1990).

[6] "Religion at Boston University." http://www.bu.edu/religion/faculty/bios/prothero.html (accessed on July 24, 2009)

[7] Prothero, 164, 217.

[8] Davis, 16.

level is rising, the earnings gap is widening, origins of immigrants are changing, people and jobs are spreading outward and regional differences are diminishing. "The scattering of families to geographical distant areas has been a significant factor in the rising popularity of cremation. Costs for transporting a dead body from Europe to the United States exceeds (sic) $2,500 while the journey from Asia can go as high as $3500."[9]

In countries like Japan and Singapore, space is very limited and cremation is often practiced out of practical necessity.[10] During an interview with a Japanese Christian leader, when the author questioned him about burial modes for those in his community, he was surprised that a debate even existed, since he thought that cremation was absolutely acceptable. Christians in Japan, due to the scarcity of space, cremate the body following the Christian service; it is not at all a pagan practice for them. Their faith in resurrection is but in the power of God to call forth the dead to be resurrected regardless of the mode applied for disposing of the dead body to ashes that have been either scattered or put in an urn.[11]

---

[9] *Ibid.*

[10] *Ibid.*, 76-77.

[11] Shinji Nakagawa, Interview, April 29, 2009.

In South Korea, "Protestant Christianity and Catholic Christianity have campaigned to support a new funeral culture based on cremation."[12] Cremation is not rejected now even among mainline denominations such as the Anglicans, Lutheran and Catholics.

> The church of England is satisfied that this method of disposing the earthly body [i.e., cremation] is not contrary to the Christian doctrine of resurrection and is to be commended as fully acceptable by Christian sentiments...but Christians taught by their religion to honor the earthly body and to use it only to the glory of God, must be greatly concerned, that its committal to destruction, whether by burial or cremation, shall be as seemly and reverent as possible and shall always be accompanied by a religious ceremony.[13]

A brief history describes the change in the Catholic Church's view on cremation:

> Early papal edicts forbade cremation and considered those who practiced it to be enemies of the church...The edict stood until July 5, 1963, it was then, when an instruction from the Vatican removed the penalties that were placed on Roman Catholics who were cremated...The change was

---

[12] Park, Chang-Won. "History of cremation in Korea," in Encyclopedia of Cremation. Eds. Douglas J. Davies and Lewis H. Mate. Burlington: Ashgate Publishing Company, 2005.

[13] Irion, 121.

brought about because the reasons individuals used for cremation were space, economics, war, and hygiene; none of which were focused on denying the doctrines of the church.[14]

The Lutheran Church Missouri Synod has stated their position in favor of cremation:

> Not too long ago, the church viewed cremation negatively. Because the general public associated the practice with heathen religions and/or an attempt to disprove the possibility of the resurrection, Christians were reluctant to consider it. "In itself, the practice has no theological significance and may be used in good conscience.[15]

Thus Christians in Euro-Western countries and some South-East-Asian countries, like the ones mentioned above, are turning to cremation in light of the realities of war, space, hygiene and economy. These are examples of contextual theology, as Bevans has rightly paraphrased Bouillard that "a theology that is not somehow reflective of our times, our culture, and our current concerns—and so contextual—is also a false theology."[16]

---

[14] Davis, 54.

[15]The Lutheran Church Missouri Synod: What is the Missouri Synod's position on cremation? *http://www.lcms.org/pages/ internal.asp?NavID=2124* Accessed on September 3, 2009.

[16] Bevans, Models of Contextual Theology (Maryknoll, New York: Orbis Books, 2005), 5.

Conclusion

This work has examined the traditional burial mode of the disposal of the dead in the last rites, showing that Indian Christians need a contextual theology of cremation in the current adverse circumstances. The increasing challenges of social pressure, scarcity of land, uncooperative neighbourhoods and biased local-government bodies have created opportunities to examine the burial custom that, in the final analysis, has turned out to be more traditional than theological. The examination of the tradition of Christian burial has revealed that regarding burial as Christian and cremation as pagan is a misinterpretation of the Christian Scripture. It also exposes ignorance of the cultural context. A thorough examination of the traditional burial mode has further paved the way for a contextual theology of cremation. Christians do not have to suffer from feelings of guilt about losing their "Christian identity" when they opt for cremation. Now they can stand with a culturally "Indian Christian identity." In the context of India, the Christian identity is not demonstrated through the mode of burial but by remaining in the customs and culture of the land. The Christian funeral service in the cremation mode can serve as an avenue through which non-Christian friends and relatives of the Indian Christians can have the opportunity of listening to the message of resurrection and eternal life. The contextual theology of cremation is an appropriate response—both theologically and missiologically—to the current challenges posed by the traditional burial mode.

Sources Consulted

Alphonse, Martin. The Gospel for Hindus: A Study in Contextual Communication. Chennai, India: Mission Educational Books, 2003.

Bevans, Stephen B. Models of Contextual Theology Maryknoll, New York: Orbis Books, 2005.

Coleman, L. William. It's Your Funeral Wheaton, Illinois: Tyndale House Publishers, 1979.

Davies, J. Douglas. Cremation Today and Tomorrow. Bramcote, Nottingham: Grove Books Limited, 1990.

_____, with Mates, Lewis H. Encyclopedia of Cremation. Aldershot: Ashgate Publishing Ltd., 2006.

Davis, John J. What About Cremation: A Christian Perspective. Winona Lake, Indiana: BMH Books, 1989.

Dupree, Stephen Wesley. "Discovering a Contextual Model for Training Japanese for Cross-Cultural Ministry" PhD diss., Asbury Theological Seminary, Wilmore. K Y, 2004.

Dyrness William A., Veli-Matti Karkkainen, Juan Francisco Martinez and Simon Chan, eds., Global dictionary of theology: A resource for the Worldwide Church. Downers Grove, Ill: IVP Academic; Nottingham, England: Inter-Varsity Press, 2008.

Fraser, James W. Cremation: Is it Christian? Neptune, New Jersey: Loizeaux Brothers, 1965.

Griffin, Emory A. A First Look at Communication Theory, 7th Ed. Boston: McGraw-Hill Higher Education, 2009.

James, E. O. Prehistoric Religion. New York: Barnes and Noble, 1963.

Hill, Jeff and Peggy Daniels. Life Events and Rites of Passages: the Customs and Symbols of Major life-Cycle Milestones, Including Cultural, Secular, and Religious Traditions Observed in the United States. Detroit, MI: Omnigraphics, 2008.

Irion, Paul. Cremation. Philadelphia: Fortress Press, 1968.

New King James Version: 1979, 1980, 1982.

Pandey, Raj Bali. Hindu Samskaras: Socio Religious Study of the Hindu Sacraments. Delhi: Motilal Banarsidass, 1969.

Pawson, J. David. Explaining The Resurrection. Kent, England: Sovereign World, 1993.

Prothero, Stephen. Purified by Fire: A History of Cremation in America Los Angeles: University of California Press, 2001.

Rush, Alfred C. "Death and Burial in Christian Antiquity" Ph.D. Diss., The Catholic University of America Press, Washington, D.C., 1941.

Smith, Donald Kent. Why Not Cremation? Philadelphia: Dorrance & Company, 1970.

Vaux, Roland de. Ancient Israel: Social Institutions Vol.1 New York: McGraw-Hill Book Company, 1965.

Wigoder, Geoffery. *The New Encyclopedia of Judaism*. New York: New York University Press, 2002.

INTERNET SOURCES

British Broadcasting Company News. "Hindu Fights for Pyre 'Dignity'."
    2009,   *http://news.bbc.co.uk/2/hi/uk_news/england/
    7960489.stm*, 2009 (accessed on March 26, 2009).

———————, "South Asia Thousands mourn missionary's death."
    http://news.bbc.co.uk/2/hi/south_asia/261391.stm. Accessed
    on September 2, 2009.

"Chennai Christians Consider Cremation." 2004, *http://
    www.indiamike.com/india/india-travel-news-and-commentary-f80/
    chennai-christians-consider-cremation-t7813/*, May 1, 2009).

Creech, Mark. "Is Cremation Christian?" in The Raleigh World, 2002,
    *http://www.worldnewspaperpublishing.com/News/FullStory.asp?
    loc=TRW&ID=367.* (accessed   May 1,2009).

IBN Live "Paralytic burnt alive in Kandhamal Violence." http://
    ibnlive.in.com/news/paralytic-burnt-alive-in-kandhamal-
    voilence/ 75439-3.html. Accessed on September 2, 2009.

"How Do People Greet Each Other in Greek?" *http://wiki.answers.com/
    Q/How_do_people_greet_each_other_in_Greek,* (accessed
    September 2, 2009).

Sar News, "Don't bury your dead here, Manipuri village heads warn
    Christians," *http://www.indiancatholic.in/news/storydetails.php/
    12811-1—Don%E2%80%99t-bury-your-dead-here, - Manipuri-
    village- heads-warn-Christians.* (accessed September 4, 2009)

Siddharth, Gautam. "Christians taking to cremation in a big way." *http://
    /timesofindia.indiatimes.com/articleshow/msid-2374986,prtpage-
    1.cms* (accessed September 4, 2009).

Sharma, Subhash C. "Cremation and Its Origin in Hinduism." 2008.
    *http://seva.sulekha.com/blog/post/2008/03/cremation-and-its-
    origin-in-hinduism.htm* (accessed December 30, 2009).

The Lutheran Church Missouri Synod: What is the Missouri Synod's position on cremation? *http://www.lcms.org/pages/internal.asp?NavID=2124* Accessed on September 3, 2009.